MAYA & MIGUEL

Grace

NEIGHBORHOOD FRIENDS

Crystal Velasquez

SCHOLASTIC INC.

New York   Toronto   London   Auckland   Sydney
Mexico City   New Delhi   Hong Kong   Buenos Aires

ISBN 0-439-73384-7

Designed by Rick DeMonico

12 11 10 9 8 7 6 5   15 16/0

Printed in the U.S.A.
First printing, August 2005

Part One

FRIENDS FOREVER?

Chapter One

Besides spending time with my family, nothing makes me happier than being with friends. Luckily, my twin brother Miguel and I have great friends — and they're always ready for whatever incredible adventures we can dream up.

Take Theo and Andy. Miguel is always hanging out with them. And my best friends Maggie and Chrissy and I are a lot like the Three Musketeers. You know, "All for one and one for all!" That's why we have a special name for ourselves. *Una, dos, tres . . . ¡Las Tres Amigas!* We're all different, but together we make a great team!

Although there was one time when our team fell apart, and we were more "all for none."

One day, we decided to open a lemonade stand in front of our apartment building. Chrissy helped me set up the table and Maggie spread a beautiful tablecloth over it. Even Paco pitched in. He perched on my shoulder while I opened a big cooler and took out a plastic pitcher. Then Chrissy dumped a bag of lemons and limes on the table.

I rubbed my palms together, ready to get started. "All right, it's almost time for us to open for business. I've practiced my sales pitch . . ."

"I have my secret recipe," Chrissy added, smiling.

Maggie held up a giant sign in front of her. "And I planned out the advertising campaign."

Among the three of us, we had everything covered. I just knew it would be a great day!

Chrissy didn't waste any time. She squeezed some lime juice into the pitcher. Too bad the first squirt went right into my eye. Ouch!

"*¡Cuidado!*" I cried, rubbing my eye.

Chrissy winced. "Oops, sorry. I have to really squeeze the limes to get out all the juice."

"Whoa," Maggie cut in. "Did you say limes? I made a sign for lemonade." She turned her sign around so I could see. I had to smile at the line of happy, dancing lemons Maggie had drawn. They even had little shoes and top hats.

"It's beautiful!" I said. Maggie is so talented.

She shrugged. "But it doesn't have limes. Can't we just make plain old lemonade?"

Chrissy shook her head. "No. Sometimes lemons and limes like to be together with their best friend, sugar. In the Dominican Republic, we put lime juice in our drinks." She finished squeezing a few lemons and limes into the pitcher already filled with sugared water. Then she poured a freshly made lemon/limeade and handed the glass to Maggie.

Maggie took a dainty sip and licked her lips. I guess it was pretty delicious, because Maggie made a quick decision.

"Okay, I'll add a dancing lime," she said. She laid her sign on the ground and started drawing a happy dancing lime right in the middle of the lemons.

Let's see . . . what else would we need? Oh, right! I took out a stack of plastic cups and put them on the table. "Get the napkins, Paco."

"*¡Servilletas!*" Paco squawked. "Coming right up!"

Miguel and his friends turned a corner onto our street, kicking a soccer ball back and forth to one another.

"Hey, look what the girls set up," Miguel said, kicking the ball toward Andy.

Andy's eyes bugged out and he licked his lips thirstily. "A lemonade stand!" He kicked the ball to Theo.

"Where?" Theo said, his eyes lighting up. When he turned to look at the lemonade stand, the ball bounced off his backside and flew into the air like a comet! It spiraled way up into the clouds then slowly started falling . . . straight at our stand!

"Look out!" Theo yelled.

All of our hard work was about to go down the drain!

Chapter Two

C hrissy, Maggie, and I all looked up at the same time to see the ball sailing toward us. I could already picture it smashing into our stand and sending happy little lemons and limes flying. But just in time, Miguel flew up out of nowhere and grabbed the ball in his hands. Phew! We all sighed in relief.

"Nice save!" Andy said, patting Miguel on the back.

Miguel smiled at Andy, then he turned to us. "So how much for some lemonade for your hero?"

"For the hero, it's free. For you . . ." Maggie joked.

I bumped her playfully with my hip. "Actually, it's free for you and all your friends."

Chrissy poured a glass and held it out to Theo.

"Weren't you guys supposed to be working on your book report today?" Theo asked as he reached for the cup.

Chrissy snatched the drink away. "Except you."

"What'd I say?" Theo asked.

Miguel pulled Theo to the side and whispered, "Never remind them of homework they're supposed to be doing." He came back to the stand, where he and Andy downed their drinks in two giant gulps.

"*Aaaah* . . . thanks!" they said at the same time. Theo just stared at their empty cups.

"Look at that," Maggie said, her arms crossed. "They drank their lemonade even though Theo didn't have any."

"*We* would never do that," Chrissy declared.

Miguel shot all of us a look. "You took Theo's drink away because he mentioned homework!"

"That's not the point," said Chrissy huffily.

"The point is," Maggie jumped in, "that we stick together."

"No matter what," I finished. "Nothing will break *us* apart."

Right on cue, Maggie and Chrissy yelled, "All for one and one for all!"

"*¡Todos para uno, y uno para todos!*" Paco squawked.

We posed back to back and raised our arms. "*¡Las Tres Amigas!*"

Andy smirked. "Here we go again."

"What?" I asked.

Miguel stood between Theo and Andy and puffed his chest out. "Just so you know, we stick together, too. All the time. I mean, look at us. We're part of a team." They were all wearing their soccer uniforms since they were on their way to practice.

"Yeah," Theo chimed. "We're like a well-oiled machine."

Andy delivered the knockout punch. "And we did *our* homework already!"

With that, the three boys zoomed off.

"Boys!" Maggie sighed.

I started to add something, but as much as I hated to admit it, the boys were right. "Um . . . maybe we should do our homework? We only have a week before we give our book report."

Chrissy shrugged sheepishly. "Yeah. I haven't even read the whole book yet."

"Don't worry," Maggie said confidently. "I've read *The Three Musketeers* at least ten times."

Chrissy shot Maggie a skeptical look. "Really?"

"Of course. It's a classic," Maggie said. Then she got a little twinkle in her eye. "And I have a great idea about how we could make our presentation really special."

Chapter Three

Later that day, the boys put their teamwork to good use on the soccer field. Andy and Theo held their own, pushing the ball down the field, while three opposing boys scattered around them, fighting to defend their goal. Andy passed it to Theo with one smooth kick, then Theo tried to pass it to Miguel, but Hector swooped in and blocked the pass. He stole the ball and shuttled it over to his teammate.

Then Miguel raced up and stole the ball! He dribbled it back down the field toward the goal, slipping it right past the goalie. Everybody cheered!

"Nice move, Miguel!" the coach yelled.

Afterward, the coach was still beaming. "Great

practice, guys." Some of the kids gave each other high fives. "Next week I'm having tryouts for a second forward. Somebody who can dribble and kick the way Miguel can."

All the boys buzzed with excitement as they gathered their stuff to leave. Miguel picked up his soccer ball and bounced it on his knees as if it were the easiest thing in the world.

"Can you sort of coach me this week?" Andy asked Miguel a little shyly. "For the tryouts for forward."

"Sure, no problem," Miguel replied, never taking his eyes off the ball.

"Thanks! Gotta go." Andy zoomed off the field just as Theo zipped in, smiling and out of breath.

"Oh, man, forward's a position I'd like to play," Theo told Miguel. "Can you give me some pointers?"

This time Miguel was thrown off his rhythm.

What should he say? He'd already agreed to help Andy. "Well, I —"

"Thanks, Miguel!" Theo interrupted happily and ran after the rest of the team.

Miguel's mouth hung open as he realized he was stuck. "Uh-ohhhhh . . ."

Chapter Four

Meanwhile, back in my living room, Maggie and I were having the most fun dress-up party ever. We each had on these fancy-looking pants and white ruffled shirts that Maggie had made. The sofa was covered with hats, plumes, belts, and all sorts of other stuff. We were going to look awesome for our school project!

"If we dress up like the Three Musketeers, it'll really add punch to our report," Maggie said. She looked down at the third ruffled shirt hanging over the chair, and then checked her watch impatiently. "Except there are only two of us. Where's Chrissy?"

Paco, who was perched nearby watching everything, squawked, "*Tarde . . .*"

It was true — Chrissy *was* running pretty late. But I just knew she'd show up any minute. "I'm sure she'll be here," I said, pacing nervously.

The door swung open. I looked up hopefully, but it was just Miguel and Andy.

"Whoa!" Miguel yelled, taking in the scene.

I admit that our living room did kind of look like an exploded costume shop.

"Why are you guys wearing caterpillars on your lips and beak?" Andy asked, smiling curiously.

"Caterpillar!" Paco cried, flapping his wings excitedly. He tried to eat the black fuzzy thing on his beak, but spat it out right away.

"They're fake mustaches," I answered, shaking my head at Paco.

"We're the Three Musketeers," Maggie told them, adjusting her shirt.

Miguel looked confused. "Without Chrissy?"

"*Squaaawk!*" Paco screeched. He thought he was the Third Musketeer.

"Sorry, Paco," Miguel said, readjusting our parrot's false mustache.

I paced a little more. "Chrissy will be here soon."

"She'd better be," Maggie huffed.

"Well, good luck," Miguel said, and he led Andy into his room. I could tell he thought we were going to need it.

Miguel needed a little luck himself. He had promised both Andy and Theo that he would help them practice for the forward position. Even I wouldn't have had an easy time coming up with a plan to get out of that one!

Back in his room, Miguel and Andy looked through a soccer book that showed all kinds of different plays. They stopped on a picture of a player doing a really fancy move with his feet.

"That is so cool," Andy said, pointing to it. "I'm going to get that move down the next time we practice."

Miguel winced just thinking about practice. Theo would kill him if he knew Miguel was helping Andy, too. "Uh, Andy, could you sort of keep our practices just between us until the tryouts?"

Andy shrugged, still flipping through the book. "Sure, okay."

"Cool." Miguel breathed a sigh of relief. At least Theo wouldn't find out. Wait . . . Theo! He'd promised to meet Theo on the soccer field for practice in ten minutes! "Oh, man," Miguel said, jumping to his feet. "I . . . um . . . left my lucky soccer towel on the field. Be right back." He tore out of there, taking his soccer ball with him, leaving behind a confused Andy.

Miguel ran all the way to the field and made it there in record time. He was huffing and puffing by the time he found Theo, sitting cross-legged on the grass, his face buried in a soccer book. Miguel almost couldn't see him behind the huge stack of books next to him.

"Sorry I'm late," Miguel said, resting his hands on his knees and trying to catch his breath.

"It's okay," Theo answered, barely pulling his eyes away from the page. "Did you know that mathematically, the best way to score a goal from the forward position is to —"

"Theo."

"Huh?"

Miguel gently took the book out of Theo's hands and replaced it with the soccer ball. "Practice, remember?"

"Yeah, sure," Theo said, a little embarrassed. He started dribbling the ball awkwardly.

"And don't tell anybody I'm coaching you, okay? Till tryouts, I mean."

"Sure, no problem."

Miguel sighed. *Maybe this won't be such a disaster after all*, he thought. But then he watched Theo kick the ball into the stack of books, which flew everywhere.

He wasn't out of trouble yet!

Chapter Five

Maggie and I had been dressed in our Three Musketeers costumes for what seemed like forever. We sprawled on the sofa on top of all the belts and hats, our mustaches at crazy angles. Maggie checked her watch for the millionth time. Chrissy was seriously late. At last we heard a knock at the door.

"Finally!" Maggie cried.

"*¡Por fin!*" Paco echoed.

Chrissy raced into the room, clutching a copy of *The Three Musketeers*. "Sorry I'm so late, guys, but —" She paused and looked at Maggie and me. "What's with the weird outfits?"

We got to our feet, straightening ourselves up. "They're Musketeer costumes," Maggie told her.

"I made them." She tossed Chrissy her outfit. "You're Aramis."

Chrissy glared at her. "What did you call me?"

"Uh . . . Aramis? One of the Three Musketeers?" Maggie said. Seeing Chrissy's confused look, Maggie realized the problem. "You haven't read the book."

A quick flash of guilt crossed Chrissy's face before she said, "Yes I have! It's just . . . maybe I should get to pick which Musketeer I want to be."

Maggie leaned back against the sofa and crossed her arms. "Okay. Which one do you want to be?"

Chrissy shifted from one foot to the other, looking anywhere but at Maggie. "The one with the sword?" she replied uncertainly.

Maggie threw her arms up and started pacing the room furiously. "Honestly, Chrissy, you always do this. And you're always late."

Chrissy put her hands on her hips, fuming. "Name one time I was late."

"Kindergarten. The 'Little Miss Muffet' recital. I was Little Miss Muffet and you were the spider. Only the spider didn't show up!"

I remembered that show! Maggie had sat onstage for at least ten minutes, swinging her legs and repeating her line over and over again. I couldn't help but giggle. "I thought that was funny."

Maggie spun around to face me. "Yeah, you and a hundred fifty other people in the audience."

"Yeah, okay, I was late," Chrissy admitted. "But as always, *you* chose the spider for me. Maybe I wanted to be Little Miss Muffet, did you ever think of that?" She planted her fists on her hips.

Paco picked up a straw and pretended to sword-fight with it. "*En garde!*"

I took the straw out of his wing right away. These two didn't need any encouragement. "All right, guys, we're supposed to be working together —"

Chrissy and Maggie both looked at me at the

same time and shouted, "You stay out of this!" Chrissy turned on her heels and headed straight for the door. "If it's going to be like this, maybe I don't want to be a Musketeer."

Now my best friends were mad at *me*, too? "But what about our book report?" I cried.

"I'm going to choose my own story and do my own report," Chrissy replied.

"But we need *three* Musketeers," Maggie pleaded.

Chrissy nodded her head toward Paco. "There are still three of you left." She stuck her nose in the air and stalked out.

After Chrissy slammed the door behind her, Maggie gathered up her things. "It was a lot of work getting all this stuff, you know," she said to me.

"What are you doing?" She wasn't seriously giving up . . . was she?

"Going home," she answered simply. "If we're

not working together, then I need to find another book for the report."

I watched her leave with her arms full of clothes. Just as she got to the door, it swung open and Miguel staggered in with his soccer ball and a towel. He looked like he had just run a marathon. Maggie almost mowed him down on her way out.

Miguel looked at me with one eyebrow raised. "*¿Qué pasa?*"

Before I even got a chance to answer, Andy walked out of Miguel's room, carrying the soccer book. "What took you so long?" he asked Miguel.

Miguel was speechless.

Luckily, Paco broke the silence. "All for one and one for all!" he squawked.

Chapter Six

How had everything gone so wrong? Miguel was in a mess helping both Theo and Andy, and my friends and I weren't even speaking to one another! "This is awful!" I told Miguel. "I've just got to figure out a way to get everyone back together."

Paco seemed to think I didn't need to. He still wanted to be Aramis. "All for one!" he screeched. He had all three mustaches on his beak in messy lines. Miguel laughed out loud, but I was way too grumpy to smile.

"Stop, Paco. You're not helping."

"*No lo puedo creer. Las Tres Amigas* broken apart just like that!" Miguel said.

I pouted and crossed my arms. "I can't believe it, either."

"Stop worrying." Miguel patted me on the back. "Maggie and Chrissy can't stay mad for too long."

"This long is already too long," I said. "Besides, how would you feel if Andy and Theo suddenly stopped speaking to you?"

Miguel smiled smugly, as if he couldn't even picture it. "That would never happen."

"Oh yeah?" I challenged my twin. "Just wait until they find out you've been coaching both of them at the same time for the same position on the soccer team."

He shrugged. "They wouldn't care."

"Then how come you haven't told them?"

Miguel blushed. "Because I —"

The doorbell rang and Miguel slumped in relief.

"*Squaaaawk!* Saved by the bell!" Paco cried.

I knew I'd made my point. "I'll get it." When I

swung the door open, there was Chrissy, carrying a big pile of stuff. "Chrissy! You're back!" Now maybe we would put all this silliness behind us and get back to being friends.

"Told you," Miguel said, smiling. He noticed the clothes and things Chrissy had in her arms. "And see? Presents."

"*¡Regalos!*" Paco screeched excitedly.

"You didn't have to," I told Chrissy, breaking into a big smile.

But the expression on Chrissy's face was all business. "I didn't. This is all the stuff I've borrowed from you." She plopped the whole mess down on the floor. "I'm giving it all back."

"Uh-oh," Miguel mumbled, looking worried.

Uh-oh was right! "But Chrissy —"

Before I could finish, Maggie came in, pulling a wagon full of things. The two of them saw each other, frowned, and moved to opposite sides of the room. "Hi, Maggie," I offered.

"*¿Regalos?*" Paco asked hopefully.

Maggie had the same all-business look on her face that Chrissy did. "I brought back all your stuff."

"Oh, no, Maggie." I groaned. "Can't we just make up? *¿Las Tres Amigas — por favor?*" Maggie didn't budge. I turned to Chrissy. "Please, Chrissy."

Neither of them even looked at me. Chrissy's eyes were on Maggie's wagon. "Hey, wait a minute," she said suspiciously. "That sweater's not Maya's. It's mine."

"And that's *my* bracelet," Maggie said, eyeing Chrissy's pile.

"And this T-shirt." Chrissy crossed over to Maggie's wagon and started picking through the stuff.

"This pen," Maggie said, crossing over to Chrissy's stuff.

"These socks," Chrissy said.

I hurried toward her. "No, those are mine."

"This book." Maggie held up a small book that I recognized immediately.

"No," I said, stepping toward her. "That was a present to me from my abuela."

Before I knew it, I was in the middle of a snowstorm of stuff. We kept sorting and exchanging and tossing things this way and that way, until I completely lost track of what was happening.

When the smoke cleared, Miguel, Paco, and I were buried in the returned things, and Chrissy and Maggie were long gone. Miguel and I poked our heads out from under the pile. Looking at all the stuff my two ex-best friends had returned made me incredibly sad. I sighed. Miguel put his arm around my shoulder, trying to comfort me.

Paco peeked his head out from under the pile. "All for one," he said limply.

I didn't know about that. The future of the Three Musketeers didn't look too bright.

Chapter Seven

I had never gone so long without talking to my friends. It was awful! Even Miguel and his friends noticed how strange we were acting the next day at school. The three of us usually sit together in class, talking and giggling. Now we sat as far from one another as we possibly could, trying to pretend the others didn't exist.

"Wow, Miguel. You were right," Theo said in awe.

"Yep. *Las Tres Enemigas*."

"Wow, enemies." Theo's mouth dropped open. He couldn't believe it.

It got even worse during lunch. I got my tray as usual and stood in the cafeteria line. When I went to reach for a carton of milk, another hand reached out for the same one. I looked up to see Chrissy. *Maybe this is her clumsy way of making peace,* I thought. I smiled a tiny smile at her, but she went right on frowning. Fine! If she was going to be like that . . . I turned away angrily.

She got back in line in a different place, just to find she was right behind Maggie! They frowned at each other, and Maggie turned away from Chrissy in a huff — only to come face-to-face with me. I tried smiling at her, but she didn't smile back. So I frowned, too. We went completely out of our way to avoid crossing one another's paths, making big figure-eight patterns around the cafeteria, finally sitting at different tables to eat. Not that I had much of an appetite.

Across the aisle from me, Miguel shook his head. "Look at them," he said to Andy.

"We'd never do that," Andy said.

Theo shook his head. "Girls . . ."

"If they were a soccer team," Miguel continued, "they'd never score a goal."

"Not without a lot of coaching." Andy nudged Miguel and winked.

"And some intense tryouts." Theo nudged Miguel's other side and winked.

Miguel smiled sheepishly but stared straight ahead. My voice kept echoing in his head. *Just wait until Andy and Theo find out you've been coaching both of them at the same time.* Miguel gulped. He was in big trouble and he knew it.

Chapter Eight

The next couple of days wore Miguel out! He would spend one hour with Andy, practicing square passes and dribbling, and afterwards he'd secretly meet with Theo. He kept up the pace at first, but pretty soon it got to be too much. Miguel started getting clumsy, tripping and falling for no reason. Between school and all the extra practicing, he was exhausted. Turns out it is hard work keeping secrets from your friends.

It got so bad that Miguel could barely remember which one of his friends he was going to practice with from one minute to the next. I hated to say "I told him so," but . . . I told him so!

What happened next was bound to happen sooner or later. Miguel ran to the soccer field to practice with . . . um, which one was it again? Theo or Andy? He just couldn't remember. "Andy?" he called out, unsure. When no one answered, he called, "Theo?" Good thing he hadn't yelled it louder, because Andy rushed in, out of breath.

"Sorry I'm late," he said, taking the ball from Miguel.

"Oh, Andy," Miguel said, relieved. "Yeah, sure. That's OK."

"Can we practice that overhead chip shot?"

"Yeah, chip shot. Overhead. Right." Miguel yawned and dragged his feet.

"Are you OK?" Andy asked.

Miguel didn't want to give anything away, so he straightened up and tried to look more awake. "I'm great. Chip shot. Like this." He dribbled the ball, but when he tried to kick it over his head, his foot slipped and the ball went flying off in the wrong direction, landing right in Theo's arms!

Andy and Miguel's eyes shot open in surprise.

"Hey, Theo. What are you doing here?" Andy asked.

Theo crossed his arms and looked suspiciously from Andy to Miguel. "What are *you* doing here?"

"Uh . . ." Andy stammered. "S-s-soccer practice with Miguel."

Miguel groaned.

"Me, too," Theo said.

"I'm trying out for forward," Andy continued.

"Me, too," Theo said.

Andy and Theo both crossed their arms and turned to my brother. "Miguel?"

Miguel blushed and smiled weakly. "Sorry, guys. I can explain. Thing is . . . both of you asked me and I couldn't say no to either of you because you're both my friends and I couldn't tell you about it because you might get mad." When he paused, he saw Andy and Theo burning with anger. "Sort of like you're getting now."

Andy was the first to explode. "How could you do this to us?"

"Yeah, how?" Theo demanded.

Miguel got more and more nervous. "Because I — you . . ." he stumbled, looking at them. All of a sudden, he got a bright idea. "Hey, why don't we all practice together? That way —"

"Forget it!" Andy yelled. "Go practice with your best friend Theo there." He stalked off the field.

"Andy, wait!" Miguel tried to call him back. But Andy wouldn't listen. "Theo?"

"Best friend? Ha," Theo said sarcastically. "That joke's so funny I forgot to laugh." Theo stomped off the field, too, leaving Miguel alone, sitting on his soccer ball. But of course it slid out from under him and landed Miguel flat on his back. He sighed.

It wasn't long before the boys exchanged every-thing they'd ever borrowed from one another, too, just like Maggie and Chrissy and I had. In the blink of an eye, Miguel and Paco were buried under a pile of clothes, baseball cards, and electronic game players. Paco squawked sadly. "*Ay, yay, yay.*"

Things weren't going any better for us girls. We avoided one another everywhere we went. We wouldn't even sit on the same bench in the school yard! It's like we were all bouncing around in these giant plastic bubbles. Things were really getting out of hand.

The next day Miguel and I sat together at lunch — but no one sat with us. We watched Maggie, Theo, Chrissy, and Andy grab their trays and sit at different tables. "Everyone's sitting apart. What are we going to do?"

"I have no idea," Miguel said.

For once, neither did I.

Chapter Nine

I may not have known what to do about our friends, but I did have to decide what to do about my report. It was due soon, so I had to get prepared. "Fine," I said to Paco as I searched through a stack of books on my floor. "If Maggie and Chrissy are going to do their own book reports, then so will I. I have lots of books right here I can pick from." I picked up one of the books. "*Little Red Riding Hood . . .*"

Paco hopped onto my shoulder and pretended to hunt me. "*Squaawk!* The better to eat you with!" He mimicked a wolf's howl.

I gave him a smile, then put the book aside. "Too young." I picked up another book. "*Charlotte's Web . . .*"

Paco shuddered and flapped his wings wildly. "Pigs and spiders — yuck!" He landed on my head.

"Paco! *¡Ya!* Settle down," I begged. I dropped the book and sighed. "All I really want to be is a Musketeer. . . ." I wiped my face with my hand. "It's so hot in here."

Suddenly my ponytail holder lit up and started going crazy! Aha! There was one thing that could turn my new worst enemies back into my old best friends. "*¡Eso es!* Lemonade!"

By that afternoon, I had everything I needed to reopen the lemonade stand. Everything, that is, but my best friends. Paco did his best to fill in, but it just wasn't the same. He spread the tablecloth over the small table but it was all crooked. Then he opened the sugar container and by accident poured sugar all over the table. I wasn't much better. I opened the cooler to take out the cups, but the lid knocked right into Paco and sent him flying! Then I tried squeezing the lemons into the pitcher, but the other lemons started rolling off the table. *¡Qué lastima!* This wouldn't be as easy as I had thought!

Paco and I had just started chasing after the lemons when we saw Chrissy. "Chrissy, Chrissy!" Paco squawked, sounding as relieved as I felt.

"Hi, Paco," Chrissy said quietly.

I gave her a shy smile. "Hi, Chrissy. What are you up to?"

"Stuff," she said, trying to sound casual. But I could tell she wanted to help.

"It's hard running a lemonade stand with just Paco," I complained. I paused nervously. "Do you want to do it together?"

Chrissy smiled right away and exclaimed, "Okay, I'll get some limes!" She took off like a shot. I was still watching Chrissy run to get the limes when Maggie showed up.

"Hey, lemonade again."

"Uh-huh," I said, smiling.

She hesitated for a second, and then asked, "Do you need help with the sign?"

"Yeah, could you?" Maggie got right to work as if she'd just been dying for me to ask. But then Chrissy came back with the limes. "Oh . . . Chrissy," Maggie mumbled.

"Hi." Chrissy sounded nervous.

Maggie started to step away. "Maybe I'd better —"

"Don't go," Chrissy spoke up quickly, touching Maggie's shoulder. "I like it best when we're all together."

"Even though I'm bossy?" Maggie asked.

"And even though I'm late?" Chrissy added.

"And even though I'm in everyone's business?" I finished.

Maggie smiled. "Yeah . . . we go well together. Like peanut butter and chocolate . . ." Chrissy and I gave her a weird look. ". . . I mean, jelly."

"*Arroz con habichuelas*," I said.

"Dogs and fleas!" Chrissy offered. Now it was our turn to give Chrissy a weirded-out look. Chrissy just shrugged. "It was the first thing I thought of."

Maggie giggled. "I think what Chrissy's trying to say is that sometimes lemons like to be with . . ."

Chrissy caught on right away. "Limes . . . and their best friend . . ."

"Sugar!" I yelled happily. "So . . . we're best friends again?"

We all smiled at one another and I knew that we were.

had finally made up with my friends, but Miguel still had some work to do. It had been days, and Theo and Andy still weren't speaking to him or to each other!

Without his friends to talk to, soccer practice wasn't much fun for Miguel. He stood alone and practiced keeping the ball in the air with his feet and knees. He stopped and looked around for Andy. Miguel saw him kick the soccer ball toward the goal, just like they'd practiced, only it soared outside the right post. "Whoa!" Andy yelled.

Miguel felt sorry for him. If they were talking, he would have told Andy that he just needed to angle his foot a little to the left. But since they weren't friends now, he looked around for Theo instead. Theo was practicing his dribbling. He was doing OK, too, until he did a fancy twist in the air and wound up stepping on the ball. He fell to the ground with a thud and the ball plopped down in his arms.

Miguel had some advice for Theo, too, but since they weren't talking, he had to keep it to himself. Just thinking about that made him so mad that he started dribbling the ball faster and faster. Theo and Andy must have thought he was trying to show off, because they started dribbling faster, too. Pretty soon, they all dribbled down the field from different directions, and kicked their soccer balls toward the goal. The three balls sailed through the air, smashed into one another, and then landed side by side on the ground.

Miguel, Andy, and Theo ran to where the balls had dropped. My twin bent down and picked up a ball.

"Hey, that's my ball," Andy argued.

"No, it's mine," Theo said.

Miguel got really angry. "I know my soccer ball when I see it," he said.

"Yeah, right." Andy snatched it out of his hands and pointed to a dark spot on the bottom. "So what about this smudge? That's my smudge."

"No, it's my footprint," Theo said, grabbing for the ball.

"This is my soccer ball!" Miguel hollered and started pulling on the ball, too. All three of them yanked on the soccer ball until it scooted right out of their hands. The boys landed on their backsides while the ball plopped down and rolled to a stop beside the other two balls. They all looked at one another, and then at the soccer balls, and just burst out laughing!

Miguel got up first, and reached down to help up Andy. Then Andy reached down and pulled up Theo.

"I'm sorry, guys," Miguel said. "I really am."

"Me, too," Theo said.

"Me, three." Andy gave them an embarrassed smile.

"So then what are we waiting for? You guys have tryouts tomorrow!" They each took a ball, paying no attention to whose ball was whose. "Square pass, back pass, overhead chip shot," Miguel called out. Now that they were friends again, Miguel would make sure both of his friends could be great forwards.

Finally, the day of the tryouts came and the competition was tougher than ever. Everybody cheered from the sidelines while Hector dribbled the ball down the field. He took a shot at the goal, but missed by a mile. Then an even bigger player dribbled it down toward the other goal, but kicked it out of bounds. At last, Andy and Theo got to strut their stuff. Andy took possession of the ball and dribbled it down the field. He made a cool back pass, and when someone passed it back to him, he caught it with one foot and made a totally awesome overhead chip shot right into the goal!

Theo made a great play, too. He slipped when he was dribbling the ball and almost lost it, but he recovered just in time to make a sharp, off-balance shot that zipped past the goalie and went right into the net.

After the tryouts, the boys gathered around Coach Carlos. "All of you did such a great job!" Coach said, beaming with pride. "As for our new starting forward, well, I was so impressed that I'm changing our formation to accommodate two new starting forwards: Andy and Theo."

Everybody cheered and Miguel and Andy and Theo gave one another high fives. Miguel was really happy that they had done so well. But he was even happier that they were friends again.

They weren't the only ones. After Maggie, Chrissy, and I got back together, the Three Musketeers did, too. Our report could not have been better! At the end, we saluted with our fake swords and everybody clapped. We took off our giant hats and bowed. It felt great to be reunited with Maggie and Chrissy.

I guess just because you're best friends, it doesn't mean you'll never have a fight. But when you're angry, it's good to remember why you were friends in the first place. Like the Three Musketeers said . . . all for one and one for all!

Chapter Eleven

It was almost dinnertime in our house and the food smelled delicious. I helped set the table while Papi chopped vegetables and Mamá stirred a big pot of rice. Even Paco chipped in, dropping napkins at every place setting. Mamá looked at the table and smiled. Everything looked perfect, except . . . "*¿Donde esta Miguel?*" she asked.

I didn't even have to go looking for him. I knew exactly where he'd be — in front of the TV, playing a video game. "Oh yeah, you want some?" he growled at the screen.

I tried to get his attention, but he was way too into the game to notice.

"Eat my laser blasts, robot villain!"

"Miguel?" I asked. Nothing. Okay, this was getting ridiculous. "*Miguel!*" I yelled at the top of my lungs. But he wouldn't stop playing. So I took matters into my own hands.

"Take that, you — *hey!*" he cried. The picture on the television screen disappeared into a tiny dot. Miguel looked downright horrified. "My game!"

I stood on one side of the TV holding the plug I had just pulled. "*Es hora de comer,*" I said.

He stayed mad at me for that all through dinner. "I was just about to beat Theo's high score!" he said, grumpily picking at his food.

"You can go back and play after dinner," I said.

"I can't go back and play 'cause I didn't save my game before you killed it."

Mamá nudged his plate with one hand. "*Miguelito, come algo.*"

Miguel shot me an angry look. "I lost my appetite."

Wow. Was a silly video game really that important to him? Suddenly I felt very sorry for my twin brother. "*Pobre Miguelito.*"

He looked confused. "*¿Pobre?* Why?"

"The video game world has taken over your life."

We faced each other, nose to nose. "That's not true!"

Paco shook his head. "*No es verdad . . .*"

I just shook my head sadly. "*Si, es verdad.*"

Paco flew over to me and landed on my shoulder. "Yes. It's true."

"Nuh-uh," Miguel said.

"Yuh-huh."

We continued the argument at school the next day.

"Nuh-uh!" Miguel said, walking down the busy hallway. Theo kept quiet, trying to stay out of it.

"Yuh-huh!"

"So I like video games. *¿Y qué?*" Miguel stopped to face me.

"Like them?" I laughed. "You play them constantly!"

Theo finally spoke up, trying to lighten the mood. "Maya's right. Too many video games can rot your brain."

Miguel narrowed his eyes at Theo. "You just don't want me to beat your high score!"

"Well, that too — but I'm really worried about you, man. Maybe you should get some new hobbies."

The bobbles on my ponytail holder lit up and shook as I thought up another idea. "Hobbies! *¡Eso es!*"

"*Eso* no *es*," Miguel said huffily. "I have lots of hobbies." He counted on his fingers. "Sports, drums, drawing . . ." There was a long pause. It was pretty clear that was the whole list. "Um . . ." He scratched his head.

Theo and I smiled at each other.

"Maybe you should try knitting," Theo suggested with a wink. "My grandma could show you —"

"You stay out of this!" Miguel yelled.

"Just trying to help you out with your problem, Santos."

Theo may have been joking, but I still thought finding Miguel other hobbies was a great idea. I decided I'd help Miguel get over video games for his own good!

Chapter Twelve

That night after dinner, Miguel headed straight for the TV. He grabbed his video game controller and turned it on — but the screen stayed black. *Weird*, he thought. He opened the system and found that it was empty. Empty!

"*Maya!*" he screamed. He came stalking into my room, steam coming out of his ears. "Where are they?"

I ignored his question and instead held up two potted plants. "Wouldn't you like to join me in planting these daisies? Gardening is a great hobby!"

Miguel fumed. "I want my video games back," he said quietly.

"*Lo siento, hermano,*" I replied. "I can't do that."

Miguel turned red and stormed out of the room yelling, "*Mayyaa!*" This tough love thing was going to be hard.

But Miguel would not give up video games without a fight. Later that night, Miguel brought Paco into the living room. "OK, boy, smell the game! Smell the game!"

Paco sniffed the case.

"Got the scent, boy?" Miguel asked hopefully.

"Got it! Got it!" Paco squawked.

"*¡Bueno!* Now . . . go find my game!"

Paco flew around the room, like he knew exactly where he was going. He veered left . . . then right . . . then stopped, pointing at the refrigerator like a retriever.

"The fridge," Miguel said, impressed. "I should've known. Ooh, she's good." He opened the refrigerator and rifled around inside. "You sure it's in here, Paco? I don't see it."

"Left," Paco directed. Miguel moved his hand to the left.

"More . . . more . . ." Paco said. Then, *"Squawk!"*

Miguel pulled out what his hand had stopped on: half a sandwich. "Paco, this is —" Before Miguel could finish, Paco swooped in and snatched the sandwich out of his hand.

"¡Gracias!"

Miguel fumed. *There's got to be a way to find my game,* he thought. *No way am I going to beg Maya!*

Chapter Thirteen

"**P**lease?" Miguel begged.

Even though I felt bad for Miguel, I had to say no. I shook my head.

Miguel dropped to his knees and clamped his hands together. "*Pleeeeaaaaaaaasssee?*"

I sighed. "It's worse than I thought." I put my hand on my brother's shoulder. "You'll thank me later."

That's when Miguel exploded! "Why are you always meddling in other people's lives?"

Ouch! I took a step back. "Meddling? I help people."

"*¿Ayudas?*" he asked, as if he couldn't believe I really thought that. "Ha. Your problem is you think people need your help, when it's really just meddling."

Even Paco agreed! He nodded knowingly and said, "Meddling. Meddling."

I shot Paco a look. "I do not!"

"You couldn't stop meddling even if you tried."

Now it was my turn to get mad. "Name one time I meddled when it wasn't necessary."

Miguel raised one eyebrow at me. "Okay." He whipped out a small notepad from his pocket and flipped to a page. "Ahem," he began. "February sixteenth. Remember Abuela and Señor Felipe?"

My eyes popped open really wide. How could I forget? I could see it now. . . .

Señor Felipe and Abuela stood in the room I had decorated. Bubbles filled the air. Bolero music blasted in the background and the disco-ball lights spun so fast, they made me dizzy. It was meant to be romantic, but I think it just gave Abuela a headache.

"What's going on?" Señor Felipe wanted to know.

"I'm not sure, but I have an idea," Abuela said. "¡Nietos!" *There was no point in hiding anymore. Abuela was onto us. I pushed open the door and came out, then leaned back in and pulled Miguel out, too. Abuela just raised an eyebrow and said,* "I knew it."

Okay, so I had been wrong that time. But I meant well, trying to fix up my abuela with the mailman. I laughed nervously. "I still say she was lonely . . ."

Miguel nodded as if to say, *Yeah, right.* Then he flipped forward a few pages in his notepad. "Mmm hmm. What about April second? Remember my baseball card?"

I could practically see that day in my mind like a movie . . .

The baseball player Orlando Flores broke into a

sprint, running as hard as he could away from the weird-looking moose that was chasing him — also known as me and Miguel.

"*Wait, you don't understand!*" *I called after him. Then I turned to Miguel who was behind me inside the stuffy moose costume.* "*Come on, Miguel. ¡Corre! ¡Corre!*" *We chased him even faster, and the crowd cheered.*

Orlando started zigzagging all over the park as if he were running from a swarm of bees. But I wouldn't give up!

"*I can't see anything, Maya,*" *Miguel had complained.* "*No puedo ver. Why are we running?*"

"*¡Vamos! He's getting away!*" *I cried, ignoring Miguel.*

"*Espera, Maya. Slow down! I can't hold on! Mayyyaa!*" *Miguel shouted. But I kept running faster and faster. Finally, I pulled away and the moose costume came apart.*

Okay, maybe that hadn't been my best moment,

but I had been on a mission! "You did get that autograph," I reminded Miguel.

"But we had to dress up like a moose to get it!"

"Whatever."

Miguel flipped to another page in his notepad. "June seventh. The bus stop affair."

I slumped, guilty as charged. I had seen an old woman leaning on a cane, standing on a street corner, and I thought she needed to cross the street. So I hurried her across, only to find out she'd been waiting for a bus on the opposite side, and I'd made her miss it!

All right. So maybe I had done all those things. But I was only trying to help. I frowned at Miguel. "I can't believe you wrote all that down."

Miguel crossed his arms, gloating. "Face it, you're obsessed with meddling. You couldn't stop if you tried."

I crossed my arms, too. "I can stop sooner than you can stop playing video games!"

"Ha! Want to bet?" Miguel asked.

"Yeah," I replied. "I'll bet!"

"*¡Perfecto!*" Miguel said, obviously so sure he would win. "You stop meddling, and I'll stop playing video games. Whoever breaks first has to do all the chores for two weeks."

"Deal!" I said eagerly. I thrust out my hand and we shook on it. "*Tu, ningun juego y yo no me meto.*"

Paco shook his head. "*¡Ay, ay, ay!*"

Chapter Fourteen

"Who can name one product that we get from South America?" Mrs. Langley asked in class the next day.

Miguel wasn't paying any attention to her at all. He was so busy scribbling in his notebook that he didn't even look up. Mrs. Langley came up behind him and asked, "Miguel? Is there a problem?"

Miguel jumped in his seat, totally embarrassed. "Oh! Hi. Heh." He tried to cover up what he'd been scribbling, but Mrs. Langley had already seen it and scooped it up. It was a video game scene with robots and spaceships.

"Very nice, Miguel . . . but we're here to learn."

"Ah . . . what was the question again?" Miguel asked, turning red.

Mrs. Langley faced the rest of the class. "Who can help out Miguel?"

Right away, my hand shot up. "I can —" But then Miguel shot me a hard stare and I remembered the bet. Whoops! I clamped both hands over my mouth. "Mpf . . ."

"Go on, Maya," Mrs. Langley said sweetly. "Help your brother out."

I clamped my hands down even harder and shook my head. No way was I going to let Miguel win that easily. Especially when I could see him staring at me, tapping his pencil and grinning, waiting for me to slip up. I whimpered, sweat beads pouring down my face. Mrs. Langley finally gave up and turned toward the rest of the class.

"Anyone else?" she asked patiently.

Theo raised his hand. "Chile has a burgeoning grape industry."

I collapsed facedown on the desk and gave a huge sigh of relief.

When we got home from school, Miguel shot me a cocky grin. "Almost had you there. You were ready to meddle."

I put my hands on my hips. "You're so into video games that you were drawing them in your notebook!"

Miguel laughed as if that were nonsense. "Yeah, right. I haven't even thought about video games all day!"

But after I stalked out, something called to Miguel.

"Miguelito, why have you deserted me?" Miguel turned to see where the voice was coming from. But it just couldn't be . . . the TV had formed a face and it was talking to him! "I miss you! We used to have such good times together!"

Miguel looked longingly at his old friend, while the screen flashed images of spaceships and robots. "Remember this?" the TV asked. Miguel gulped. He could hear the familiar beeps and bloops, drawing him in. He drifted closer to the TV . . . luckily, he snapped out of it just in time.

"No!" Miguel cried, shaking his head. "I don't need you! You're not going to get the best of me!"

He ran out of the room, but he could still hear the TV calling to him. "Wait, don't go! Remember all those high scores? Miguel . . . you can still beat Theo if you really try. . . ."

Chapter Fifteen

Neither one of us said a word during dinner. Mamá noticed that we weren't our usual chatty selves.

"How was school today?" she asked, hoping to get us talking. "Miguel?"

He shrugged silently and mumbled, "OK."

"Maya?" Mamá asked me. I just smiled weakly and muttered something about school being fine.

Mamá and Papi exchanged worried looks. "Maybe you need to forget about this silly bet," Mamá said. "It's making you both unhappy."

Miguel and I looked up at the same time. "No!"

"We're good!" I promised.

"¡No *problema!*" Miguel agreed.

We smiled at each other, trying to pretend we were fine. But that night, I knew we weren't fine at all. I had a nightmare that I was in our family's pet store, watching Papi struggle with a big bag of dog food.

"Maya, can you please . . . *help me?*" Papi cried piteously.

I was on the floor playing with a puppy, but I turned to help right away. "Of course, Papi. Here let me —" But my feet wouldn't budge! Something had me frozen in place. "*I can't move!*" I said, panicking.

"Maya! *¡Ayudame!*" Mamá shouted from the other side of the store. I saw Mamá reaching over a fish tank to clean a filter when suddenly the fish tank grew and grew . . . until it was enormous and Mamá toppled in with a splash!

"Mamá!" I tried to move again, but couldn't. I heard a crash behind me.

"Maya, over here!" Papi cried. He was trapped under the giant bag of dog food!

"Maya! I need help!" All of a sudden, I was in Abuela's kitchen. Her sink was overflowing. The room filled up with water in seconds until it looked like a pool!

"Maya, help me!" Was that Miguel? I looked around and saw my brother standing high up on a tightrope, juggling bowling pins. He was wobbling so much, I just knew he would fall, but there was nothing I could do!

"Help Paco!" our parrot squawked. Oh, no, not Paco, too! Suddenly I saw Paco trying to land a jet plane in a thunderstorm. Poor Paco! I tried and tried to move my feet, but they were glued to the spot. The harder I struggled, the louder the whine of the engine got, until —

"Aaaaaggggh!" I woke up in my bed, sweating bullets.

Down the hall, Miguel was having a nightmare, too, which he told me about first thing the next morning. In his nightmare, he found himself standing in a world that looked a lot like one of his video games. He was just looking around when — *Blam!* — a laser blast hit the ground right next to him. He glanced up to see a flying robot swooping down over him, firing globs of slime that went *splat* as they landed. They missed him, but not by much.

"Help!" Miguel yelled as he took off running. "*¡Socorro!*" He raced down the hall, ducking blasts of slime.

"Miguel!" A computer version of me sat on top of a wall, waving at him. "*¡Hola!*"

Miguel reached out to me. "Maya! *Ayudame . . .*"

But I just shook my head sadly. "Sorry, can't meddle."

The robot plunged down and picked up Miguel

with his claws and swooped him up into the air. Miguel let out a high-pitched scream that finally woke him up. He opened his eyes to see that he was safe in his own bed, breathing hard. He lay back down.

But no way could he go back to sleep.

Chapter Sixteen

The next day at lunch, all of our friends could tell we hadn't slept. We both had pretty big bags under our eyes.

"What happened to you guys?" Theo asked.

"Nothing," Miguel and I said at the same time.

"My mom says a slice of frozen eel will help get rid of those bags under your eyes," Maggie whispered helpfully.

But Miguel and I didn't feel like reliving our nightmares again by explaining them. "Just go back to telling us about your big problem," Miguel said, getting everyone's attention back on Maggie.

"OK, OK," she said. "So I accidentally entered this dance competition on Saturday."

Chrissy looked confused. "You entered a dance competition by accident?"

"No. The accident is that it's the same night as my uncle's wedding."

"Ohhh," Theo said, nodding. "So what're you going to do?"

Maggie bit her bottom lip nervously. "I have to figure out a way to go to both."

Miguel turned to me and gave me a sly smile. "If only there were someone here who could come up with a big idea. . . ."

All eyes turned to me.

I smiled innocently. "Why are you all looking at me? I don't have any ideas at all!" But like always, my ponytail holder gave me away. The bobbles on it started flickering and flashing like a pinball machine.

"Aha!" Miguel cried. "You do too have ideas!"

"I didn't say anything!" I protested. But my hair

bobbles wouldn't stop flashing. Miguel raised an eyebrow at me. "You want me to stop thinking, too?"

Miguel couldn't argue with that. *Thinking* of ideas had not been part of the bet. Satisfied that I hadn't lost yet, he turned back to the table. "OK, how can we all help Maggie with her problem?"

But Maggie wasn't ready to give up on me. "Come on, Maya," she pleaded. "You *must* have an idea."

I was getting nervous. If I didn't leave soon, I would lose the bet for sure! "I don't have any ideas. Mm-mm. Nothing. Zip. Nada. Oops, look at the time. Gotta go."

"Why?" Miguel teased. "We're just trying to figure out how to help Maggie with her problem."

I just kept tap-dancing away, humming a tune as loud as I could. "Can't hear you . . ." I tap-danced right out of the cafeteria.

Chrissy watched me dancing my way out of the lunchroom. "She's acting so weird."

Miguel puffed out his chest. "Don't worry, Maggie. *I've* got a plan."

"You?" Maggie asked suspiciously.

"Sure. Here . . ." Miguel grabbed a napkin and started sketching on it.

"You're drawing," Maggie noted. "What are you drawing?"

"It's a plan," Miguel said confidently.

Maggie looked unconvinced. "Maya doesn't draw *her* plans."

Chrissy jumped to her feet and said, "I'm going to check on Maya."

She found me in the girls' bathroom, trying to take the ponytail holder out of my hair. It was still flashing like crazy.

"Stop it! Stop! It!" I told it angrily.

"Maya?" Chrissy asked, poking her head around

the door. Perfect timing! I grabbed Chrissy and pulled her into the bathroom.

"Chrissy! *¡Ayudame!*"

"Of course I'll help you. What's the problem?"

I told her all about the bet and how hard it was to stop meddling!

"*Sí,*" Chrissy said sympathetically.

Now came the only plan I was allowed to come up with — one to help myself! I held up a big roll of gauze bandages. Chrissy gulped.

"*Hazlo,*" I said.

Chrissy hesitated, then took the roll and got started wrapping my head.

Chapter Seventeen

Mamá had just plumped a sofa cushion and settled into the living room when I burst through the front door.

"*Hola, mi amor* —" she started to say, but when she saw me, she pulled back in shock. "*¡Ay! ¿Pero qué es esto?*"

I had made Chrissy completely cover my head with the gauze, so it looked like I had on a huge turban.

"It was the only way, Mamá."

"Ay, Maya, you're taking this too far."

But I could still feel my ponytail holder glowing through the gauze. I shook my head sadly. "*No puedo* . . . the week is almost over. I could still win!"

Paco flew in squawking, "Pretty hat! Pretty hat!" He grabbed one end of the gauze and unrolled it, spinning me like a top!

"Whooooooooaaaaah!" I fell into a chair, now without a turban. The pinball machine on my head went nuts. I sighed. "It's no use. I'll never win."

Mamá shook her head kindly. "*Ay, mi amor.* You'll feel better after you've had dinner." She went into the kitchen.

I sat on the floor, sulking. "I'm never going to win this bet! I just keep thinking of too many ideas. . . ."

But then I got my best idea yet! I saw Miguel's video game peeking out from under the sofa. I reached under and pulled out the disk. "*¡Eso es!* Miguel's video game!" I slowly loaded it into the game console near the TV and grabbed a controller. The game beeped as I moved the robots this way and that way.

As I got more and more into the game, the flashing lights on my head slowed down — then stopped altogether.

Chapter Eighteen

I completely lost track of time while I played the video game. I pleaded with the screen, "Come on, Mr. Robot-man!"

Miguel raced into the living room and stopped in front of the television. "Maya!"

Was he crazy? I had to lean over to look around him. "Move!" I said impatiently. He stepped out of the way and I kept playing.

"Maya, I have to talk to you."

"Can't talk. I've almost beaten Theo's high score."

Miguel narrowed his eyes at me. Then just like that, he pulled the plug on the TV.

No! My eyes went wide with horror. "Why'd you do that?"

"Because that's just a dumb video game!" Miguel said. I could tell by his voice that he was serious.

"Did you say 'dumb video game'?"

"Maya, this is an emergency!"

Miguel explained Maggie's problem and how he had tried to help, but it hadn't gone quite right. "*Por favor, Maya* . . . I really messed things up for Maggie and I need you to help me fix it."

I narrowed my eyes suspiciously. "You're asking for my help because you want me to lose the bet!"

Miguel shook his head. "No, I'm not! I don't care about the bet!" I must have looked like I still didn't believe him because he continued. "I'll forfeit and do your chores for a week — I just need your help."

Hmm . . . he really must need my help if he was willing to do my chores. "How about two weeks?" I asked.

"A week and a half, but no garbage," he answered.

"Deal. So what's the problem?"

Miguel unrolled a big blueprint across the floor with a flourish.

I raised an eyebrow. "You made a blueprint?"

"It was a very complicated plan," Miguel said. "I just wanted everything to go perfectly . . . but it didn't."

I shook my head. "Rookie mistake. Nothing ever goes perfectly. Murphy's Law."

"Murphy's Law?" he asked.

"Anything that can go wrong, will. You have to be flexible enough to change your plan just like that." I snapped my fingers.

I could tell Miguel was impressed by my take-charge attitude. "How was I supposed to know? Anyway, you're the expert."

I smiled and crossed my arms. "I'm the expert, huh? Okay, show me your plan."

Chapter Nineteen

"*Pssst!*" I whispered through the window of the ladies' room at the reception hall. Maggie, who was decked out in a glittery peacock dance costume, ran over to the window. She'd been hiding in the bathroom.

She gasped happily when she saw me. "Maya! I knew you'd come to save me!"

"Miguel told me about your problem," I explained. My twin was standing guard a short way down the hall.

"You have a plan to fix everything, right?" Maggie asked.

"Of course."

"Good . . . but hurry. I'm supposed to be onstage in ten minutes!"

That didn't give us much time, but I knew just what to do. "Stay here until you hear the signal. Then go out into the ballroom."

Maggie looked worried. "But everyone at the wedding will see me dressed like a peacock!" Maggie gestured at her peacock outfit, complete with a big tail-like train and a feather headdress.

I just smiled. "Leave everything to me." I rushed away from the window and Miguel followed me down the hall.

"Wait! What's the signal?" Maggie called after us.

"You'll know it when you hear it!" I yelled as I ran away.

I entered the hotel ballroom where the dance competition was being held. I got there just in time to see a dancer with a number on her back finish an elegant turn, bow, and walk out of the room. I grabbed some equipment I'd placed there beforehand and rushed right out onto the floor.

"Excuse me, ladies and gentlemen," I said in a deep voice. The spotlight swung over to land on me and the hardhat I'd just put on. "Sorry to interrupt the competition, but we've got some code issues." I looked down at a clipboard, pretending to flip through some paperwork.

"What code issues?" one of the judges asked.

"Oh, you know . . . the usual ones. Really bad stuff . . . so bad that I shouldn't even tell you. So everyone needs to leave this room right away."

They weren't too happy about that. "But we're in the middle of a dance competition!"

"Yeah . . . well, sorry," I said, making my voice even deeper, "but you're gonna have to move to the ballroom next door."

The judges shared puzzled looks, and then shrugged and got to their feet. I couldn't believe it! My plan was working like a charm!

"All right," the female judge said. "As long as we can continue the competition."

The male judge squinted at me. "Either I need new glasses, or these building inspectors are getting younger every day."

After they left, I said into my walkie-talkie, "Peanut butter, this is banana. The salt has left the shaker."

Chapter Twenty

"Roger that, banana," Miguel said from the wedding reception ballroom. He watched as the confused judges filed into the room, looking around at all the wedding guests.

The male judge paused to take a canapé from a tray on a nearby table. "Oooo, this room has *hors d'oeuvres*!" He turned and spied the beautiful three-tiered wedding cake on another table. "And cake!"

It was showtime! Miguel cupped his hands around his mouth and crowed like a rooster. *Cock-a-doodle-doo!*

Maggie, still in the bathroom, looked up. "The signal!" she said excitedly, and ran toward the ballroom.

Meanwhile, Miguel worked his way over to the

DJ station and punched a button to dim the lights. One spotlight shined on the dance floor, and music poured out of the speakers. "Ladies and gentlemen," Miguel said into the microphone, "we present to you, *Maggie!*"

Maggie spun out onto the dance floor and into the spotlight, her feathers floating behind her. *¡Qué bonita!*

The judges stopped eating, mesmerized by Maggie's dance. Her uncle and his new wife turned to look, too. They smiled and held each other's hands, touched that Maggie was performing for them.

"It worked," Miguel said, amazed.

"Hey, I know my meddling," I joked.

"This wasn't meddling. *Estabas ayudando.* Maggie wanted your help. Good job." He slapped me five.

Maggie finished her dance with a dramatic spin and the judges went wild with applause. "*Brava! Brava!*" they cried. Maggie bowed gracefully, the lights glittering off her costume and feathers drifting all around her.

The plan made everyone happy . . . including me, except that Maggie's uncle made us sweep up all the peacock feathers. As for Miguel, he still plays video games, but not nearly as much as he used to. He's taken up knitting, after all. . . .

Just kidding!

Maya & Miguel™

¡Eso Es! Maya Doll

"¡Eso Es!"
"That's It!"

- THE 14" MAYA DOLL SAYS 10 PHRASES IN ENGLISH AND SPANISH

- MAYA'S PONYTAIL SPINS AND LIGHTS UP

- PLUS EXTRA OUTFIT AND FUN HAIR ACCESSORIES

LOOK FOR MAYA WHEREVER TOYS ARE SOLD!

SEE IT ON PBS KIDS GO!℠

pbskidsgo.org/mayaandmiguel

Toy Play™
1 East 33rd Stre
New York, NY 1001
www.toy-play.co

■ SCHOLASTIC
www.scholastic.co